# A Note to Parents and Teachers

Kids can imagine, kids can laugh and kids can learn to read with this exciting new series of first readers. Each book in the Kids Can Read series has been especially written, illustrated and designed for beginning readers. Humorous, easy-to-read stories, appealing characters and engaging illustrations make for books that kids will want to read over and over again.

To make selecting a book easy for kids, parents and teachers, the Kids Can Read series offers three levels based on different reading abilities:

### Level 1: Kids Can Start to Read

Short stories, simple sentences, easy vocabulary, lots of repetition and visual clues for kids just beginning to read.

### Level 2: Kids Can Read with Help

Longer stories, varied sentences, increased vocabulary, some repetition and visual clues for kids who have some reading skills, but may need a little help.

### Level 3: Kids Can Read Alone

Longer, more complex stories and sentences, more challenging vocabulary, language play, minimal repetition and visual clues for kids who are reading by themselves.

With the Kids Can Read series, kids can enter a new and exciting world of reading!

# Franklin's Picnic

From an episode of the animated TV series *Franklin*, produced by Nelvana Limited, Neurones France s.a.r.l. and Neurones Luxembourg S.A, based on the Franklin books by Paulette Bourgeois and Brenda Clark.

Story written by Sharon Jennings.

Illustrated by Sean Jeffrey, Sasha McIntyre and Shelley Southern.

Based on the TV episode *Franklin's Picnic*, written by Brian Lasenby.

 ® Kids Can Read is a registered trademark of Kids Can Press Ltd.

Franklin is a trademark of Kids Can Press Ltd.
The character of Franklin was created by Paulette Bourgeois and Brenda Clark.
Text © 2006 Contextx Inc.
Illustrations © 2006 Brenda Clark Illustrator Inc.

Kids Can Press acknowledges the financial support of the Government of Ontario, through the Ontario Media Development Corporation's Ontario Book Initiative; the Ontario Arts Council; the Canada Council for the Arts; and the Government of Canada, through the BPIDP, for our publishing activity.

Published in Canada by
Kids Can Press Ltd.
29 Birch Avenue
Toronto, ON  M4V 1E2

Published in the U.S. by
Kids Can Press Ltd.
2250 Military Road
Tonawanda, NY  14150

www.kidscanpress.com

Series editor: Tara Walker
Edited by Jennifer Stokes
Designed by Céleste Gagnon

Printed and bound in China

The hardcover edition of this book is smyth sewn casebound.
The paperback edition of this book is limp sewn with a drawn-on cover.

CM 06  0 9 8 7 6 5 4 3 2 1
CM PA 06  0 9 8 7 6 5 4 3 2 1

**Library and Archives Canada Cataloguing in Publication Data**

Jennings, Sharon
   Franklin's picnic / Sharon Jennings ; illustrated by Sean Jeffrey, Sasha McIntyre, Shelley Southern.

(Kids Can read)
The character Franklin was created by Paulette Bourgeois and Brenda Clark.

ISBN-13: 978-1-55337-714-6 (bound).    ISBN-13: 978-1-55337-715-3 (pbk.)
ISBN-10: 1-55337-714-1 (bound).    ISBN-10: 1-55337-715-X (pbk.)

I. Jeffrey, Sean  II. McIntyre, Sasha  III. Southern, Shelley
IV. Bourgeois, Paulette  V. Clark, Brenda  VI. Title.  VII. Series: Kids Can read (Toronto, Ont.)

PS8569.E563F765 2006      jC813'.54      C2004-906886-5

Kids Can Press is a **l⊙rus**™ Entertainment company

# Franklin's Picnic

Kids Can Press

Franklin can tie his shoes.

Franklin can count by twos.

And Franklin can eat

lots of flies.

Franklin loves flies.

Franklin's friends do not love flies.

Sometimes, this is a problem.

One day, Franklin was playing baseball.

It was his turn at bat.

"Uh-oh," said Bear. "It's twelve o'clock.

I have to go home for lunch."

"Me too," said Skunk.

"Me too," said everyone else.

"Wait till I have my turn!" cried Franklin.

But his friends all ran off.

"Phooey," said Franklin.

Franklin went home

and ate lunch by himself.

Then he ran back to the park

and waited for his friends.

He waited ...

... and waited.

By the time everyone showed up,

Franklin had a good idea.

"Let's eat lunch together tomorrow," he said.

"You mean a picnic?" asked Beaver.

"Yes," said Franklin. "I will bring the food."

"That will be fun!" said Bear.

At suppertime, Franklin told his parents

about the picnic.

"I'm going to bring the food," he said.

"What will you make?" asked his mother.

"I will make fly sandwiches

and fly cookies," said Franklin.

"Do your friends like flies?"

asked his father.

"Everyone likes flies," said Franklin.

"Hmmm," said his parents.

That night, Franklin made fly cookies.

He got out sugar

and eggs and fly flour.

He stirred in two cups

of chocolate-coated flies.

He rolled and

patted and baked.

"Mmmm-mm!" said Franklin.

"Everyone will love these cookies!"

"Are you sure?" asked his mother.

"Sure I'm sure," said Franklin.

The next day, Franklin made
fly sandwiches.

He got out a fresh loaf
of whole-fly bread.

He opened a new jar
of crunchy fly butter.

He used the last of the
cherry fly jelly.

"Mmmm-mm!" said Franklin.

"Everyone will love these sandwiches!"

"Are you sure?" asked his father.

"Sure I'm sure," said Franklin.

Franklin got out the cooler.

He packed the sandwiches and cookies.

Then he mixed up a jug

of fly syrup and water.

"This will be a wonderful picnic!"

said Franklin.

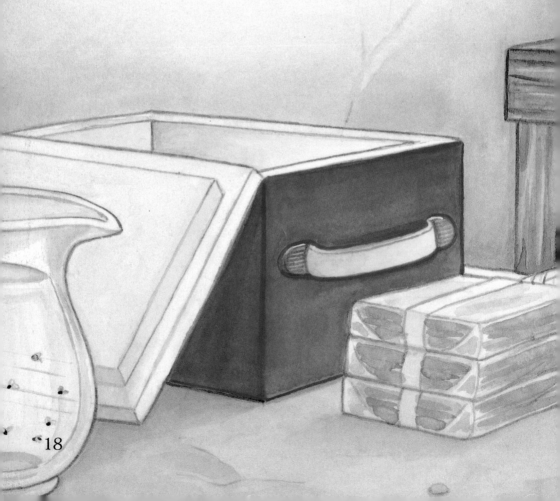

19

Franklin and his friends

played baseball all morning.

"I'm getting hungry," said Skunk.

"I'm starving!" said Bear.

"So am I," said Beaver.

"Me too," said Rabbit.

"Then let's start
our picnic!"
said Franklin.

Bear spread a blanket
on the ground.

Beaver got out
plates and cups.

Rabbit and Skunk ran for the cooler.

Franklin put out

the food.

Everyone sat down.

"What did you make, Franklin?"

asked Beaver.

"Fly sandwiches and fly cookies

and fly juice," said Franklin.

"Uh-oh," said Skunk.

"I hate flies," said Rabbit.

"Me too," said everyone else.

"I like ants," said Beaver.

"Me too," said everyone else.

"But flies are good!"

said Franklin.

Franklin helped himself to lots of food.

The others watched.

Franklin took a big bite of his sandwich.

"Mmmm-mm!" he said.

The others frowned.

"Oh, come on,"

said Franklin.

"Just try a little bite."

"Well," said Bear.

"I am hungry."

The others nodded.

Everyone took a sandwich.

Everyone took a little bite.

Everyone chewed and swallowed.

Then everyone said, "YUCK!"

Just then, Franklin's mother came by.

"Is anyone still hungry?" she asked.

"I brought a pizza."

"Pizza!" everyone cried.

"Are there flies on it?" asked Beaver.

"No," said Franklin's mother.

"Just ants."

Everyone had two slices.

Except for Franklin.

"Ants?" he said. "YUCK!"